FROGGY'S DAY WITH DAD

FROGGY'S DAY WITH DAD

by JONATHAN LONDON

illustrated by FRANK REMKIEWICZ

SCHOLASTIC INC.
New York Toronto London Auckland Sydney
Mexico City New Delhi Hong Kong Buenos Aires

For golfers Sean, Matthew, Abby & Max,
Uncle Chris & Bill, and Mr. Frazier, too.
(And for my son Aaron, who gave me the mug.)
　　　—J. L.

For Larry, Phil, Monica, Bill, Artie, Jim, Rick, and Nick, who all enjoy a good game.
　　　—F. R.

ISBN 0-439-72986-6

Text copyright © 2004 by Jonathan London. Illustrations copyright © 2004 by Frank Remkiewicz. All rights reserved. Published by Scholastic Inc., 557 Broadway, New York, NY 10012, by arrangement with Viking Children's Books, a member of Penguin Group (USA) Inc. SCHOLASTIC and associated logos are trademarks and/or registered trademarks of Scholastic Inc.

12 11 10 9 8 7 6 5 4 3 2 1　　　　5 6 7 8 9 10/0

Printed in the U.S.A.　　　　　　　　　40

First Scholastic printing, May 2005

Set in Kabel

FRROOGGYY! called his mother.
"Wha-a-a-t?" cried Froggy.
"Rise and shine," said his mom.
"It's Father's Day!"

"Hurray!" cried Froggy.
He hopped out of bed
and flopped to the kitchen—*flop flop flop.*

He'd been waiting a long time
for Father's Day to come.
At school he'd made a special present.
And now he was making breakfast for Dad
all by himself.
He dropped an egg on his foot—*splat!*
"Oops!" said Froggy.

FRROOGGYY!

called his dad.
"Wha-a-a-t?"
"What's that funny smell?"
"You'll see!" said Froggy.

Then he served his dad
breakfast in bed.
"Happy Father's Day!" said Froggy.
"I made it all by my—oops!
It slipped!" *Splat!*

"Oh, Froggy," said his mom.
She scooped it up
and Froggy's dad took a bite.
"Mmmmmmmm, thanks, Froggy," he said.
"The eggshells are nice and crunchy."

"I have another surprise for you!"
said Froggy after breakfast.
"We're going to play golf! For Father's Day!
It's your favorite game."
"You're too little to play golf," said Dad.
"But you're just the right size
to play *miniature* golf."
"Yippee!" said Froggy. "Let's go!"
"First you have to get dressed, silly!"

"Oops!" said Froggy.
And he flopped back to his room to get dressed—*flop flop flop!*

zap!

zip!

zim!

zoop!

zup!

zat!

"I'm *re-e-a-dy!*" cried Froggy.
And he and his dad leap-frogged all the way
to the fun park—*flop flop flop.*

"First," cried Froggy, "let's ride the bumper boats!"
"Okay," said his dad. "Then we'll play golf."
Froggy sat on his dad's lap
and helped steer—*whip-splash! whip-splash!*—*oof!*

They bumped another boat so hard
that Froggy bounced up into the air—*"Wheeeeeeeeeeeee!"*...

turned a somersault . . .
and landed upside down in the boat—*thump!*

"Let's go to the batting cage!" cried Froggy.
"Okay," said his dad. "Then we'll play golf."

Froggy put on a helmet—*zat!*
Then he wound up and swung—
"Oops!" The bat flew out of his hands . . .
and hit his dad in the foot—*thunk!*

"Now can we play golf?" asked his dad.

"Golf?" said Froggy. "Why didn't you say so? Let's go!"

So they flopped over to play miniature golf—*flop flop flop.*

At the first hole, Froggy wound up and started to swing . . .

FRROOGGYY !
yelled his dad.
"Wha-a-a-a-t?"
"You're facing the WRONG W-A-A-A-Y-Y!"
"Oops!" cried Froggy. "I knew that!"

Froggy turned around.
Then he wound up and started to swing. . . .
"Wait!" said his dad.
"First, you have to address the ball."

"Oh," said Froggy. "Hello, ball!"
"No!" His dad laughed. "I mean,
stand with your feet apart
and place the head of the club
behind the ball—*then* swing."

Froggy shrugged,
then wound up and swung—

and landed in the hole—*plop!*
"Hole in one!" cried Froggy.

After his dad's turn
(it took *him* NINE TIMES to hit the ball in—
and Froggy said, "Nice try, Dad!")
they flopped to the next hole—*flop flop flop*.

"Now watch *me!*" said Froggy.
And he wound up and swung—
  Bam!
    Bing!
      Boing . . .
The ball bounced off three towers . . .

and hit his dad smack in the head—*bonk!*—
and knocked him down.

"Ooops!" cried Froggy,
looking more red in the face than green.
"Thanks, Froggy," groaned his dad.
And he rubbed a bump on his head
the size of a golfball.

The rest of the game was fun though—
especially for Froggy.
He dove into a pond beneath a waterfall—
flop flop . . . *splash!* . . .

and came up with seven balls!

And when they got back home,
Froggy gave his dad
his special Father's Day gift.
"Happy Father's Day, Dad!"

His dad tore off the paper—*rrrrriiiiippp!*
"Wow! A mug!" he said.
"Yep!" said Froggy. "I painted the letters
all by myself. It says: *To the Best Dad I Ever Had.*"

"Thanks, Froggy!" said his dad.
"This is the best gift
I ever had!"